PRAISE FOR *LAST MESSAGE* FROM **SEVEN (THE SERIES)**

"Part mystery and part adventure…a fantastic and thrilling page-turner…Highly Recommended."
—*CM Magazine*

"Amusing and suspenseful." —*Kirkus Reviews*

"[The] adventures are exciting and readers will be anxious to pick up the next book in the series."
—*NJ Youth Services*

PRAISE FOR *DOUBLE YOU* FROM **THE SEVEN SEQUELS**

"This thrill-a-minute series will hook…fans of James Bond and Jason Bourne."
—*School Library Journal*

"A romantic spy thriller with a heart."
—*Kirkus Reviews*

"Teen readers who know and love the James Bond stories and movies will enjoy the novel and find many similarities and intricacies linking back to Fleming's work within the storyline."
—*CM Magazine*

SEPARATED

SHANE PEACOCK

ORCA BOOK PUBLISHERS

Library and Archives Canada Cataloguing in Publication

Peacock, Shane, author
Separated / Shane Peacock.
(The seven prequels)

Issued in print and electronic formats.
ISBN 978-1-4598-1164-5 (paperback).—ISBN 978-1-4598-1165-2 (pdf).—
ISBN 978-1-4598-1166-9 (epub)

I. Title.

PS8581.E234S47 2016   jc813'.54   c2016-900492-9
                             c2016-900493-7

First published in the United States, 2016
Library of Congress Control Number: 2016933640

Summary: In this middle-grade novel, Adam finds
himself alone and on the run in Sweden.

*Orca Book Publishers is dedicated to preserving the environment and has
printed this book on Forest Stewardship Council® certified paper.*

Orca Book Publishers gratefully acknowledges the support for its publishing
programs provided by the following agencies: the Government of Canada
through the Canada Book Fund and the Canada Council for the Arts,
and the Province of British Columbia through the BC Arts Council
and the Book Publishing Tax Credit.

Design by Teresa Bubela
Cover photography by Alamy.com
Author photo by kevinkellyphotography.com

ORCA BOOK PUBLISHERS
www.orcabook.com

Printed and bound in Canada.

19 18 17 16 • 4 3 2 1

To Ernest and Vernon, best grandfathers.

"I never cry," said Pippi.

—ASTRID LINDGREN, *PIPPI LONGSTOCKING*

ONE

I hate it when Mom calls me *sensitive*. I'm a guy. I'm almost a teenager. I can't be a twelve-year-old boy and sensitive at the same time. That's not possible. But as I stood in that crowd, not a single face familiar to me for as far as I could see, my lifeline cut, fear making my knees weak, and my heart pounding like a basketball rattling hard inside a hoop, I knew she was right on the mark.

I was alone. I had *never* been so alone. And I had never been so frightened in all my life.

Just two days earlier, I had been safe and sound—sort of. And Grandpa and I were on a plane a million miles above the Atlantic Ocean. That's the "sort of" part. How can you even be remotely safe when you are inside a steel object weighing about a trillion pounds that is hanging in the air, or at least hurtling through it, and might at any second fall out of the sky and send every last person inside it to a fiery death, arms and legs ripped off, heads severed and blood splattered all over the place and…perhaps I shouldn't go on. I won't even mention the remains-getting-eaten-by-sharks part. Not that I'm sensitive.

Grandpa sure isn't. I can picture him now, sitting there next to me in our economy-class seats (not a big spender, is David McLean) and looking highly insensitive. That doesn't sound right, and I don't think I mean it the way it came out. He's a good man and a caring grandfather and just about perfect in every way, even though he's old. Sometimes I actually wish he wasn't so perfect. I doubt he talks to himself inside his head like this. But at that moment on the plane he looked like he didn't have a care in the world: a real guy, strong and manly and bold.

We were on our way to Sweden, which, at the time, was a good thing, and I was about to barf, which obviously wasn't. I had my attention on the throw-up bag in the pocket of the seat in front of me, eyeing it sideways so he couldn't tell I was looking at it so lovingly. I'm not a good flier. Never was and never will be. Grandpa, on the other hand, is among the best in the history of the world, the universe, the Milky Way and beyond—World War II hero and all that goes with it, pilot of every plane known to mankind and for many years the operator of what he called an import/export business. I could never figure out what that really was and what he really did. But he flew all over the world doing stuff. And now that he's retired, he's still flying all over the world…doing stuff. He has lots of friends in all parts of the globe, and he likes to visit them.

A while back he stopped in at our house in Buffalo and offered to take me on one of his trips to celebrate my *becoming a man*, as he put it, and clapped me so hard on the shoulder that I just about fell over. He'd made similar offers to all six of his grandsons and had already followed through on a few. What he meant by *man* was a teenager, a thirteen-year-old. I was still a few months from that then, though I'm almost there now. But age was beside the point—the chance he gave me to go far away, to the land of IKEA and the world's best meatballs and other cool things, was something I was into immediately.

I should have been in school, it being the first week of September and all. That was an added bonus when he made the offer (and maybe helped blind me to the fact that I was going to have to fly in an airplane to go on this trip). From way up there in the plane, the weather outside (or at least down below) appeared amazing. We were high above wispy, white clouds that looked like massive stretched-out cotton balls, and the sky was clear blue all around us. I use the word *sky* loosely, because as far as I could figure out from the altitude the pilot said we were at, we were basically in space. That meant that when we started to fall, we'd reach terminal velocity really quickly. Maybe we'd die before we even hit the ocean, before the plane ripped into the water like an atomic bomb into concrete, disintegrated and evaporated all of us.

But there was Grandpa, disgustingly calm, sitting beside me with his black beret still on his head, smiling at me every now and then (and each time I gave him my best fake smile back), his earbuds in and music pumping out of them. Yep, I said *pumping*. This guy is God knows how old—I've lost track, but he's over eighty for sure—and he was listening to the Black Eyed Peas or something like that. It sure sounded like "Boom Boom Pow." I knew he was a Frank Sinatra fan—he always slapped me hard on the back when he had that sort of historical stuff ramped up on his stereo. My cousins tell me they've heard him listening to lots of Elvis too and even the Boss, Bruce Springsteen. This guy is so open-minded it is sickening. He'd obviously found some channel on the music feed on the plane that was giving him newer stuff, and he'd just started getting down. And, of course, he was multitasking. I guess when you've flown dangerous missions in a war and been all over the world doing amazing things like climbing mountains in your spare time, you've got to have that sort of talent.

He was reading, and he'd been at it just about all the way across the ocean…as he nonchalantly flew in that deadly machine, listening to music and smiling at me.

Reading? Not exactly my idea of a scintillating time. I wished I had my cell phone with me—or at least the cell that would finally be mine on my thirteenth birthday.

Grandpa was some sort of speed reader too, of course. He must have read about three or four books on that flight. He handed me *The Little*

Prince when we boarded (along with *another* hard clap on the back). That novel was a big fave of his, one he had read to me and all the cousins over the years. I didn't entirely get it, really—a story, almost like a fable, about this weird person, this small prince, from another planet who was involved in a plane crash. Perfect! A plane crash! I only pretended to read it as I sat there worrying. Grandpa had already read the Sherlock Holmes thriller *The Hound of the Baskervilles*— which actually sounded kind of cool, with a massive dog with glowing eyes and murder and all that stuff—and had almost finished a Swedish crime novel, which he'd started plowing into about halfway into the flight. He was kind of holding the cover away from me, and I had the feeling that maybe the story inside was a bit inappropriate for someone my age, maybe a tad violent and all. You wouldn't think the famously happy-go-lucky Swedes would be up to that sort of thing—I certainly didn't—but they actually were. Big-time. I'd done some research about them on Mom's laptop the week before we left, and it actually kind of freaked me out.

That should have been my first clue that this trip to Sweden was going to be a whole lot scarier than I ever could have imagined.

TWO

I had expected to find all sorts of information online about how wonderful Sweden was, and I did for a while. The stuff I found talked about ABBA, cool furniture and architecture, hip clothes, nice safe cities and hockey (or *ice hockey*, as they called it, which would really make my Canadian cousins barf), and how there were so few poor people and how the government paid for all your medical bills, and the fact that they had a king. The whole place was very liberal too, which would upset lots of Americans, since if you call yourself a liberal in my country, many of us (not my parents though) seem to think you're a two-headed monster or something. A few sites said Sweden was something like Canada in terms of its weather and landscape, which was fine with me since I'd often visited my cousins and Grandpa in the Great White North and almost felt at home there. I'd also been to his cottage, way, way north, and I just loved it, hanging with the guys, swimming and going on hikes. Though I'd never tell them this, I think Canada is a really neat place, really safe and friendly, though Canadians are a little laid-back and kind of secretive in some ways...which leads me back to Sweden.

The last thing I read online was an article called "The Land of Secrets—The Sweden You Never Thought Existed." It was a long story from a newspaper or magazine, something from some famous publication in New York, and I was just going to give it a pass—I hate reading long things. But man, after I read the first paragraph, I couldn't stop.

It was that article that got me started worrying about where we were going.

What this writer was trying to say was that Sweden was a much more ominous place than its reputation indicated, that its people were like icebergs—different on the outside than on the inside, with darker lives and ideas than the rest of us even imagined. They were also really open about sex (inappropriate!) and violence and not always very pleasant. During World War II they had sort of been on both sides, supplying arms to the Nazis and to the good guys, making money off them killing each other by the millions. And man, they could really make weapons. They had this wicked thing called the Bofors gun that did some serious damage throughout the war. Even the Swede who has the Nobel Prizes named after him, a dude named Alfred Nobel, was into weapons. He invented dynamite! The Peace Prize guy! And he was the head of a huge armaments company too. The only reason he came up with the prizes was that a journalist once called him "The Merchant of Death" (which was true), so out of pure guilt he created the award. Talk about deceptive, about not being what you say you are!

And the Swedes were well hooked up to the secret service and espionage world too. I suppose they were perfect for it—nice, calm people but full of hidden schemes. Even one of their greatest heroes, this guy called Raoul Wallenberg, who risked his life to help Jewish people escape the Nazis in Hungary during the war and is revered around the world, apparently was a spy. Rumor has it he was working for the CIA! The bad guys from the Soviet Union picked him up as the war wound down, and he ended up in a prison in Siberia, kept there forever, until he rotted or died or whatever. They weren't about to let him out. Not a Swede with the abilities he had.

And I couldn't believe this—one of their prime ministers, perhaps their most famous one, a really liberal guy named Olof Palme, who looked kind of boring, like a principal or something, was assassinated in the streets of their capital, Stockholm (where we were going!), right in broad daylight on one of their safe and perfect streets just after he'd gone to a movie with his wife! This wasn't in the Dark Ages— it was in 1986! And on top of that, they never really caught the guy who did it, though there are all sorts of rumors about who it was and who he was working for and what Palme was up to behind the scenes. It was amazing! Like something you'd see in a documentary with scary music, lots of bass and drums. And to top it all off, I also read that the guy who may have shot him is, in some ways, considered kind of cool in Sweden. Wow!

Another one of their great people was this guy with a completely unpronounceable name— Dag Hammarskjöld! (Dag? Really?), who was the second secretary-general of the United Nations. He died in mysterious circumstances, going down in a plane crash in Africa—just falling out of the sky for no reason. He was one of the most powerful people in the world at the very moment of his death and had his hand on all sorts of secret information.

What sort of a place were we really going to? Was it simply full of lovely people with cheerful, hip ways who sat drinking lattes in cool cafés on cobblestone streets surrounded by amazing buildings? A place of good clean "ice hockey" and ABBA ("*You are the dancing queen...oh yeah!*")? Or was it this "land of secrets" where you had to be very careful? As I said, I started worrying, and then I worried even more. Not that I'm sensitive.

Grandpa had never really made it clear what he was going to do in Stockholm. He would have been a good Swede. He kept giving me those smiles—sly ones, really. He was excellent at them. I noticed the title of that book he held in his hand, though he kept subtly trying to pull it out of my line of vision. I could see that it was about murder. And I noticed the word *secret* on the back of it in a long blurb about the plot. That was another thing I'd read about the Swedes. They didn't just write the odd dark crime novel; they wrote piles of them, and they were *really* good at it. It made me think there must be way more crime in Sweden than anyone was letting on.

I kind of like gruesome murder stories too, though my parents don't know it. I sneak a look every now and then at some of the crime shows they watch. Funny how they say they are "inappropriate" for me and yet they are so into them, even talking about them when they are making dinner. There's one called *Wallander*, which they've just started watching and seem to absolutely adore. It is particularly gross, as far as I can tell, with lots of blood and horrible crimes and has really creepy music. I remember sneaking a look at the description on the DVD case. It is set in Sweden.

Somehow I didn't unload my guts onto Grandpa's lap all the way across the ocean. I'm not sure how I did it. We Americans aren't like Swedes or Canadians—we show our feelings.

But, being a guy, I thought it important to hold on—to the death if necessary.

Then the plane started its descent into Stockholm.

It looked all right down there...at first.

THREE

I couldn't complain about our first few days in Sweden. Man, it was fun. At least, once we'd gotten out of the sky. We flew in over Scotland and then Norway and landed at Stockholm Arlanda Airport, which is way north of Stockholm. Grandpa got us a cab, and we made the long trip down to the city. I couldn't believe how much Sweden seemed like Canada at first as we sat in the back of the cab looking out at a four-lane highway with lots of Canadian-type trees on either side and a few stretches of farmland and then some modern-looking suburbs. Everything seemed awfully clean too, just like the Great White North.

Grandpa was pointing things out—he'd obviously been here many times before—smiling away at me again as I now genuinely smiled back (since we had returned to planet Earth).

When we finally got off the highway, we hit this street called Sveavägen (with two dots over the second "a"), and things began looking a little more like I figured Sweden should look. The buildings just somehow seemed kind of Swedish, not American or even Canadian. For a start, they looked older and more colorful than North American buildings, and they didn't have as much glass or even brick. They were kind of IKEA-like inside as far as I could tell from peering through the front windows. There were lots of cafés and trees, everything was very green, and, of course, most of the signs were in Swedish (though I was surprised to see some in English too). As we got down into the main part of the city, the buildings got higher and more American-looking, more like we'd come to the business district of an important urban center. I recognized some American stores and brands too.

Then something kind of spooked me.

We slowed in traffic, and I noticed that a cross street was called Olof Palmes gata. I looked the other way and saw a little tunnel-like street across from it called Tunnelgatan. It didn't have any traffic on it, since it was just for walking, and the ground was covered with some sort of square gray bricks. It was awfully narrow, and I could see, in the shadows at the far end of it, steps that led up toward another street. I had the weird feeling I'd seen this place before. And it felt like it was a bad place, for some reason. Then it hit me. This was where that Swedish prime minister Olof Palme was gunned down. It must have been *really* close to here, perhaps at this *very* spot. And Tunnelgatan was the street down which the mysterious murderer had fled! Everything in the Swedish streets had seemed so perfect until that moment, so sunny and wonderful and safe.

Our cab moved again (driven by a huge blond guy, who I realized hadn't said a single word since we'd gotten in). I must have been turning a little white, because Grandpa, who had been blabbing on about Swedish architecture, suddenly stopped the lesson.

"Aren't you feeling well, Adam?"

"I'm...I'm fine, Grandpa." I tried to give him a smile. No weakness. As I've said, Grandpa is a good guy, but something about him makes you not want to show any weakness in his presence.

"It might be a little jet lag," he said.

"Yeah, now that you mention it, it was a long flight and I feel a little...off?"

He put his hand on my shoulder, this time gently, looked a little concerned for a while but soon launched back into his lecture. I let his voice fade into the background (which is something I do often—Mom says I'm practicing to be a man) and watched the Swedes walking along the street. I told myself they didn't look too scary. And it was true. In fact, they looked awfully ordinary—

fashionable but ordinary. Then one of them caught my eye.

It was a girl. I'm not really into girls yet, but this one stood out, mostly because she was weird. I didn't get a really good look at her because she was in a crowd and down a street, but I could see she was riding a bicycle with a horse's head attached to the handlebars. She was wearing bizarre clothes and had startling red hair, almost orange like a lit pumpkin, strange pigtails and something on her shoulder that looked like a small furry human being or something. I couldn't tell. Then she totally vanished into the flow of pedestrians. I wondered if I'd made her up. I have a pretty big imagination.

Grandpa's voice was still there in the background but now getting a little more excited, like we were approaching something pretty cool.

And we were.

We turned a corner, and I saw heaven.

We had emerged into an open area near the river, one that I knew ran from the Baltic

Sea between Sweden and Finland and Europe and flowed right into Stockholm. The city was actually on several islands.

Man, it was beautiful.

"Wow, that's pretty, isn't it, Adam?" said Grandpa.

That wasn't a word I'd heard him use very often.

"I never get sick of seeing it. Maybe this will be the last time," he said.

It wasn't like him to say anything sad either, and he kind of zipped it for a few seconds after that, as if he'd said something he was thinking but hadn't intended to let out.

We turned left and moved along the water past some really stunning buildings—really old, cool places that you'd think the Vikings might have made, if they'd lived until a few hundred years ago. There was a super-old one just over an amazing stone bridge in front of us. It was massive and long, and it had a big lawn with huge trees on it, and though it appeared to be made of some sort of stone too, it almost glowed.

"That's the royal palace," said Grandpa.

I'd forgotten about that. Right, they have a king. And he lives here in the middle of the city! My buddies back home would have been really impressed.

Flowers and trees bloomed everywhere in this wide open area, and people were walking along the streets, on the bridge and next to the water— lots of blond hair shining in the sun (three-quarters of the people I'd seen in Stockholm so far were blond, which was kind of unsettling, for some reason). They all looked weirdly happy, like they were pretending, or something.

"And there's our hotel."

I couldn't believe it when I looked in the direction he was pointing. I was going to have to change my opinion about his spending habits. It was awesome and looked like it was really going to set him back a few dollars (or *kronor*, as they call the money here). And from the expression on

Grandpa's face, I had a feeling it was going to be even more impressive inside.

The Grand Hôtel was six or seven stories high and stretched along the street next to the blue water. It was a sort of reddish-brown color with a green roof, regal-looking with awnings over every window on every floor and a beautiful café that ran the full length of the building. We stopped at the biggest awning, one that extended out from the entrance, which was a set of big wide-open glass doors with shining gold borders. I counted eight gleaming wooden steps that went up into the lobby. Grandpa got out and motioned to a bellman to get our bags, then slipped him some money and we went inside.

The lobby nearly took my breath away. We were in a long room that looked like it was made for a king, as if we'd gone into the palace by mistake. There were cream-colored pillars and a huge crystal chandelier, beautiful old paintings on the walls, and a plush rug that was blue with specks of gold, Sweden's colors, which I recognized from their flag and also from their national hockey team's uniforms. Even the employees—blond, of course, and so healthy-looking it almost made you laugh—who welcomed us in English from behind an elegant, dark wooden counter and wore smart blue-and-gold ties and sleeveless sweaters.

I watched them closely, looking for hints of their dark side, perhaps hidden in their eyes. But if there was any darkness inside them, they did a good job of disguising it, smiling and calling Grandpa "Mr. McLean" and me "Mr. Murphy." I had to admit that I felt pretty grown-up.

Our room was even sicker. We went up in an elevator that appeared to be made of gold and were escorted into a big space with two rooms (I had my own!), each with a big bed and tons of pillows. The walls were cream-colored, and the drapes were bright red. Nice old paintings lined the walls here too, and there were two killer bathrooms with huge showers. (I had my own shower too!) It was somehow both historical-looking and very modern, and it was hard to tell how they'd done it. Grandpa had a gleaming wooden desk to work at, and there were three TVs! There was a big one in an area between our rooms that had a table and sofas, and a humongous one on the wall facing each bed. I almost shouted out loud, but I controlled myself.

"Will this do, Adam?" asked Grandpa as soon as the bellman left, clapping me on the back.

"I suppose we'll get by," I said, staring out the big window that overlooked the water and gave us a picture-postcard view of the Royal Palace and the Swedish Parliament on the little island across from us.

And we most definitely did get by...for the first couple of days.

FOUR

After we got to the room, we both had a shower and then considered having a nap, but neither of us was going to be able to sleep (my grandpa has more energy than people one-quarter his age), so he let me play some video games on my TV for a while. They were all awesome, and mostly in English, though I found one about Vikings in Swedish that was pretty sick too, a sort of medieval thing with a guy kind of like Thor in it, who was able to do some pretty decent damage to his opponents both while fighting from his Viking ship and while wreaking havoc on enemy villages.

He had a sword and a shield and a spear and a hammer and a little iron hat with horns coming out each side and, of course, blond hair streaming down from under his beanie, and he looked really brave and handsome—cool beyond belief. He actually looked like a nice guy most of the time, but like many Swedes, it seemed, he was wild underneath. This game had that thing where you have to achieve something and then you go to a higher and more difficult level and on and on upward. I love that idea—getting two or three dangerous missions that you have to accomplish and at the end you get a prize. Grandpa was in the other room, making phone calls in sort of a hushed voice while I played. Then he called me into his room and said we needed to talk.

"Adam, unfortunately I can't be with you all the time we are here. Will that be all right?"

"Of course, Grandpa."

What did he mean…he couldn't be with me?

"You will be alone for a few hours at a time in this room each day, but I'll let the front desk know, and I'll get them to bring up food for you, and you can play all those games you like on the TV, and I've left a stack of books for you."

He glanced toward the desk. *The Little Prince* was on top of the pile of books, but there were several Harry Potter novels too and this popular new thing called *The Hunger Games*, which I knew had a girl as the hero—I'd seen images of her on the Internet, wearing something that made her look kind of like a guy and with a bow pulled taut with an arrow in it. So there was the promise of at least a little action in that book. I tried to act like I was interested.

"So, are you okay alone with these books and food and the TV and video games?"

I tried to look a bit sad, but inside I was doing cartwheels.

"I'm thinking burgers and fries," he said, "and maybe some interesting Swedish sodas one day, perhaps some ice cream, and then possibly mac and cheese the next day."

More cartwheels.

29

"Don't worry—I'll be back in the early afternoon each day, and we'll go out and see the city. There are some great museums here with lots of Swedish history in them and some incredible art."

Cartwheels slowing drastically.

"I'll take you out on the town one night, and I've arranged to get some tickets to a hockey game on our last evening."

Back into cartwheel mode.

"Really? Like Swedish Elite League hockey?" I was hoping.

"That's right."

Good old Grandpa. He always knew how to treat his grandsons. There were lots of Swedish players in the National Hockey League back home, even a couple on my favorite team, the Buffalo Sabres. The NHL hadn't even started the season yet, but here they began earlier. The hockey in this league might not be quite as good as the NHL, but it would be close and really amazing and different. I was sure I'd recognize some players, and I'd be able to brag about seeing something that none of my buddies might ever see. I could really tease my five Canadian cousins about this. Who got to watch Swedish Elite League hockey in person? I could hardly wait. I was pumped!

"That's amazing, Grandpa!"

"I didn't tell your mom or dad that you'd have to be alone at times when we were here."

Really? I thought. You didn't tell them? Sometimes he was kind of like a kid, only a large and wrinkled one.

"But," he continued, "I thought you were up to it. You're twelve years old and will soon be thirteen, which means you'll be a teenager, and then it won't be long until you're thinking about what you'll want to do with your life. When I was a kid, I had to grow up fast. We all did in those days. I believe life gives you lots of tests, and the more willing you are to face them and rise above them, even at a young age, the better off you will be."

Ah, yes, I thought, it will be tough indeed—alone with hamburgers and fries and video games.

"I'll try to rise to the occasion," I told him with a straight face. But did he really not tell Mom and Dad about this? They are both pretty high-achieving people. My mom is a former Olympian and a very successful real estate agent, and Dad is, like, the best commercial airline pilot around, but they are pretty careful with me. Mom often says I'm sensitive as if it's a bit of a worry to her.

"This will just be our little secret. I'm sure you will be fine. Don't get me wrong. I hate the old-fashioned idea that you have to toughen up young men, and they have to be little manly men. That's not what I'm talking about here…it's just that it's good to be a little independent, to learn to not worry about things so much." He'd paused for a second and looked at me.

"I'm not a worrier," I said.

He clapped me on the back. "I know you're not. You'll be fine."

But he had me thinking a bit. Alone in a hotel with awesome food and the TV, fine, great, but alone in Sweden…land of secrets? In Stockholm, where they set the most gruesome murder mysteries on earth and assassinate their prime minister in cold blood? Stop worrying, I told myself. Sometimes I wonder if Mom is right. Maybe I really am sensitive.

Grandpa went out for a few hours that afternoon, though he waited until I was napping. I didn't get up until I heard him come in the door. I hadn't had a chance to play a single video game while he was out, which kind of ticked me off. After he got back we went down to this rather radical restaurant in the hotel, with glass tables and steel walls, and were seated almost out on the street, where we could watch the palace lit up in the distance and see people walking back and forth, everyone dressed in way more colorful clothes than people wear back home. He ordered Swedish meatballs on noodles with sauce for me and lingonberry soda. It was great.

Then it was off to bed. We were both absolutely exhausted.

When I woke up the next morning, he was completely dressed for his day, and there was a pancake breakfast with maple syrup and whipped cream and orange juice on a tray in front of me on top of the covers.

"I'll be back by one o'clock, Adam, and we'll head out for the museums then. Hang in there." The door opened and closed, and he was gone.

FIVE

It took me a while to shake off the nearly total silence in the room. All I could hear was the city in the distance. I leapt up and rushed over to the door to make sure it was locked and snapped the bolt into place to double-lock it. Then I peered through the peephole in the door and got that fish-eye view you get when you look out. The hallway was deserted. I swallowed.

"Get ahold of yourself," I said.

I steeled myself and walked back to the bed, flipped on the TV and got down to playing games, though I found it hard to play anything except that Viking thing I'd tried the day before. It got even cooler the more I explored it. Man, the things this Swede could do! Time flew by, and I forgot where I was. I must have been up to about ten thousand kills when a knock came on the door. It was sort of a sneaky knock, like whoever was doing it was testing the door, checking out who was in the room.

I was in the room. Alone.

For a moment I just sat there, trying to ignore it—maybe the person would go away— but then the knock came again, and I turned the sound off on the television. There was a long pause, then a third knock. That was the only sound in the hotel, it seemed. It was as if everyone had fled. I once saw a trailer from an old movie called *The Shining*, about a guy and his wife and kid left alone in a hotel that kind of comes alive and attacks him, and he goes insane. I thought of that for a second. Then I got up, still in my bare feet, and approached the door.

I looked through the peephole. A big man was standing there, peering back. He was unshaven and looked very serious. He knocked again, much harder. I actually jumped back.

"Mr. Murphy, I have your meal for you. Are you there?"

I felt like an idiot. I glanced down at my watch. Wow. I'd been gaming for more than two hours. It was noon.

I tiptoed into the bathroom, which was right near the door, and flushed the toilet, then called out, "Coming!"

He was a pretty stylish guy, dressed in the blue-and-gold uniform of the hotel, blond hair combed back as if a perfect wind had set it in place, and yes, unshaven but fashionably so. The meal was on a white table on wheels, and it was under three upside-down silver bowls.

"Thank you, sir," he said in the singsong, lightly accented way the Swedes speak English (and it seemed like most of them spoke it well—how did that happen?). He brought the meal right in, uncovered it, set up the utensils, poured my drink and then stepped back.

"Will that be all, Mr. Murphy? Mr. McLean wanted to be sure you have everything you need."

I glanced down at the burger bulging with cheese and mushrooms and tomatoes and lettuce, and the homemade fries with a big vat of ketchup beside them in a silver cup.

"Uh, yeah, that seems okay," I said, then felt like an idiot again. Americans can sound so dumb next to Europeans and even Canadians—kind of unsophisticated, which truly ticks me off.

Then he was gone, and I was watching TV, checking out Swedish game shows while I stuffed my face. Grandpa appeared about an hour later, blasting through the door so suddenly that I just about yelled out in shock.

"Are you all right?" he asked. "You look a little pale."

Not again.

"Must be the light," I said. That was all I could think of.

* * *

We hit the town after that. First we crossed the bridge onto the island, walked to the palace and watched the changing of the guard, which was pretty cool, with these Swedish soldiers in old uniforms and spiked helmets (not kidding) doing all sorts of maneuvers and carrying serious weaponry. Then we went right into the heart of the Old Town, or Gamla Stan, as they call it in Swedish, where everything is really old, and we walked up and down the narrow cobble-stone streets.

It felt like you could almost reach out and touch the buildings on either side. I imagined how creepy it might be in these tight streets after dark. But there were also really cool stores and cafés and people hanging out everywhere. Grandpa was treating me left and right to candy and ice cream and buying me Swedish T-shirts (*I Love Stockholm* in blue and gold) and stuff. Later, under the night lights, we saw a sort of circus without animals (not Swedish to have anybody think they were mistreating animals, I guess)—fire eating and juggling and acrobatics, all in a big ancient square.

We had an awesome time, and I couldn't help but imagine how cool it would have been to grow up here, without crime, dirty streets and all the things I was used to back in Buffalo. But I kept reminding myself that this was an illusion, that the Swedes had a dark side too. I thought about those crime novels, their dead leader in a pool of blood in the street, the weapons they made and all the stories about the secret service. Maybe many of these happy people weren't really happy at all.

I saw the girl again too, the one with the carrot-colored hair, the weird pigtails and the horse bicycle. She was on a narrow street far away and it was late at night, just before we went back to the hotel. She looked to be about my age, but there didn't appear to be anyone with her, which was strange. It occurred to me once again that I might be imagining her.

* * *

The next day Grandpa left me alone again during the morning. He didn't say a word about where he was going, and I didn't ask. It was likely just him and other adults talking anyway.

I didn't get freaked-out this time when he left nor when Sven or Mats or whatever his name was came with my meal—French toast and sausages for lunch!

When Grandpa came back he took me on a ferry ride all around Stockholm. We visited islands and stopped in for a meal of reindeer roast beef (not kidding), which was actually delicious, though it made me wonder—what kind of people butcher the beautiful animals from Santa's sleigh? Later we went on a tour of City Hall, where they hold the banquet for the

Nobel Prize awards. The building was ancient and funky, like something out of *The Lord of the Rings*. Then we checked out a museum that had a warship from the 1600s that was an absolute killing machine. And on the way home we walked past this place called Icebar—an entire restaurant made of ice. It was all a bit strange. And to add to the weirdness, Grandpa started acting a little on edge, sort of anxious, like time was running out or we were in danger... or something.

* * *

The next day, which would be our last full day in Stockholm, he went out in the morning again and returned in the early afternoon. This time he had stayed away a little longer than before, but I didn't mind, not in the least. This evening we were going to the hockey game. I had a hard time concentrating on the TV. I just wanted to get to the rink.

42

Grandpa barely spoke to me from the minute he arrived. Something serious seemed to be on his mind.

We spent a few hours in the early afternoon shopping in the commercial area in modern downtown Stockholm, which was the other way from the Old Town, heading up and down these promenades, as they call them—pedestrian streets with modern cobblestone surfaces, filled with tourist stores and fashionable places. All the clerks looked like models to me. I bought Mom and Dad a shirt each.

Then we ate some sort of fish at the hotel and got ready for the game. Though it had an early start, a six-o'clock puck drop, Grandpa seemed to be really rushing us. I couldn't figure it out. It seemed to me we had plenty of time. We'd eaten really early, just before four o'clock, and now he was pushing me to get out the door. He seemed worried.

But I didn't think too much about it, because my mind was on the game. I had dreams of being a pretty good hockey player someday, though I had doubts about my abilities. I was all right in the league I played in. I could hold my own against my Canadian cousins on the ice too, although DJ, who is the oldest and biggest, is a bit of a load out there. But I felt like a million bucks when I was on the ice with the wind blowing in my face. I felt free from all my worries. Even being near a rink, smelling it, feeling the excitement in the air, was amazing. Swedish Elite League hockey on the big international ice arena right in Stockholm! This was going to be unforgettable.

I left the hotel room that night as excited as I'd ever been. I had no idea that in a very short while it would be obvious to me that I was never coming back.

SIX

The arena was to the south, past the Old Town, in a suburban area where there was a sports park called Stockholm Globe City that had two football (that's soccer to us normal people) fields and two—count them, two—professional ice-hockey arenas.

Grandpa hustled me out of the hotel and we took a cab, even though our first stop was only about four or five blocks away, near the bottom of Sveavägen Street.

We passed a city square and drove along a street with big clothing stores like H&M and then stopped at a little glassed-in structure with a big white *T* on a round blue sign above it.

"Hurry!" cried Grandpa, and he actually grabbed my arm and pulled me out of the backseat and onto the sidewalk. What was going on?

We went inside and descended on some escalators, Grandpa actually striding down the moving steps instead of waiting for them to take him along, going so fast that I had to really move to keep up. It wasn't long before I realized we were in one of Stockholm's subway stations—the Metro, they call it. It was awfully nice, very modern, and the trains themselves were really clean, of course. But there didn't seem to be too many of them, and we waited a good ten minutes for the next one (I'd been on subways in Toronto when visiting my cousins and in New York too, and I knew that was a long wait). Grandpa stood next to me, tapping his foot nervously and looking at his watch. He seemed really anxious now. It didn't make any sense—we had nearly an hour and a half until the game started. Had they moved it to Finland or something?

"Grandpa," I finally said, "what's wrong? Why are we in a hurry?"

"Nothing," he said and looked up and down the subway platform as if searching for someone. He even looked behind us a few times. Were we being followed?

Finally, a train came and we got on with a whole crowd of fashionable and very clean and well-groomed Swedes (clothes all the colors of the rainbow) and headed south on the Green line. Grandpa seemed to relax a little.

The train was modern and sleek and almost completely silent when it moved, which seemed almost unreal. How did they do that? It was eerie.

Some of the subway stations we passed through were absolutely awesome. I'd never seen anything like them. They were like caves (and I'm a big fan of caves), though not natural ones. They were like something out of Dungeons & Dragons.

Some were blue, others red or green, and all of them were kind of glowing. It was amazing! There was lots of graffiti too—everywhere—and most was really inventive...though some was a bit inappropriate. What we were seeing, it seemed to me, was the real Swedish nature coming out.

It only took us about ten or fifteen minutes to get to Globe City, which really made me wonder what Grandpa was so worried about, because it still wasn't five o'clock when we arrived, and the game wasn't starting for over an hour.

The suburban area around the arenas was full of apartment buildings and busy roads with multiple lanes, though it was all neatly put together (of course), so it was easy to find the Globe Arena as soon as we got off the train. The Hovet Arena, which was really old and looked like a silver trashcan punched in the middle, was beside its big modern brother. Djurgårdens IF and AIK Stockholm, the two teams we were going to watch, both really famous and big rivals, played in the older rink most of the time, but tonight, to start the season (which seemed weird on such a nice, sunny day), they were going to face off in the big one. From the outside it looked awesome. It was shaped like an actual globe, a gigantic white golf ball planted in the ground in the middle of Stockholm. There was a large gathering area like a square in front of the arenas, but the crowd wasn't too large yet.

For some reason, Grandpa was still rushing us. He was even breathing hard, which was unusual for him. He took my hand, something he hadn't done for many years, and pulled me along toward the *Globen* (as the Swedes call it). It began to loom over us, casting its huge circular shadow.

Then I saw something *really* weird. There was a house, a sort of cottage, sitting way up near the top of the Globe, set there on a steep angle and just hanging from the surface! A little house!

"Look!" I said to Grandpa. He glanced up, still pulling me along.

"Oh, I know," he said. "Some artist had that put up there. The Swedes have to do things like that."

It was pretty freaky. It struck me as a symbol of being alone in the world, on a round sea of snow. Or maybe a symbol of fear—perfect for this country.

Grandpa rushed us around to the far side of the Globe and then right up to it. I could see tracks, almost like a railway line, running along the ground and up the side of the Globe, all the way to the top. Huh? I spotted a smaller ball halfway up, made mostly of glass. It was coming down along the tracks, almost hanging upside down, with people in it! What was this?

SkyView, a blue sign said.

Grandpa said something to the man who appeared to be in charge of this thing that climbed the very side of the big sphere. But what Grandpa said was even weirder.

He spoke in Swedish.

He hadn't done that the whole time we'd been here, and yet he talked to this guy really fluently, and when the guy answered him, Grandpa completely understood him. Then Grandpa seemed truly relaxed for the first time since we'd left the hotel, although, as he turned to me, he looked a little guilty too.

"Grandpa," I said, "you speak Swedish?"

"Uh, yeah, I picked a little up here and there over the years."

"But—"

"But that isn't what matters. We made it!" He glanced up at the ball that was descending the Globe toward us.

"Made what?"

"This was my surprise for you, Adam. This SkyView thing closes down at five o'clock, so it isn't running when the game is on. I was really worried we wouldn't make it on time. You are going to love this! I'm taking you up into the air to see all of Stockholm and half of Scandinavia!"

And so he did. And it was supernatural. And I almost barfed.

It was the strangest sensation, somewhere between extreme excitement and paralyzing fear. I both wanted to go way up there and dreaded doing it. I both loved every second of it and hated it. I'm kind of like that. I have sort of a double personality, almost like there are two parts to me, two different Adams. Maybe we are all like that in a way.

I turned away from Grandpa as we shot up the side of the building. We were doing something that felt absolutely impossible. The ground completely disappeared beneath our feet, as if we were hanging in the air. My stomach shot up ahead of me or stayed just behind—I'm not sure which. It was only when we got to the top and stopped that I kept my eyes open for a while. That part was a bit beyond awesome. You could indeed view all of Stockholm, probably all fourteen islands, and the old city, and the lakes and rivers and even the Baltic Sea (it seemed to me) way off in the distance. I wondered if the land I was seeing on the horizon beyond the water was actually Russia. Grandpa had been there a few times too. As the ball paused at the top, he pointed out the Old Town, the palace, the bridge over the water that led to our hotel. There it was, the Grand! But my eyes also wandered farther north toward the commercial area, the big buildings...and the spot where the prime minister had been gunned down in cold blood on the street. Why did I always have to think like that? I'm *not* sensitive.

When we got down to earth again, Grandpa took me over to a little food truck in the plaza and bought me one of the largest hot dogs I'd ever seen. I put some sauerkraut on it. We stood there eating, watching the crowd grow, filling the square now, fans moving in groups, wearing their team's colors and chanting slogans, the excitement building. But there was something kind of scary about it all too.

There were police officers everywhere. There seemed to be almost as many of them as fans, great crowds of *polis*, as they are called. They looked big and strong, and they had weapons and riot sticks.

What was going on?

"Let's go in," said Grandpa.

It was time for the game.

SEVEN

The arena was shaped like a globe inside too,
with red seats ringing the building from ground
to roof. The ice surface was huge, much wider
than at home—it looked like a frozen-over
soccer field. And there was advertising everywhere: on the boards, on the referees and even in
the huge circles around the face-off dots, which
were colored and not in dim shades—one of
them was pink!

And the atmosphere was incredible. I'd been
to one Sabres game—they'd lost to the Toronto
Maple Leafs, which really, really, really sucked—

but even at that game and in a bigger crowd than this one, the feeling in the arena wasn't anything like it was in the Globe.

First of all, the two teams, or at least their fans, hated each other. These were the two Stockholm clubs in the Swedish Elite League, after all. The Djurgårdens supporters were at one end, wearing red, blue and yellow, and the AIK's were at the other end, in black and yellow (got to have gold or yellow around these parts). And man, were they loud: singing and shouting and clapping and pointing at each other and saying what appeared to me to be nasty things. That seemed rather un-Swedish. No, it wasn't, I reminded myself.

And the cops had come indoors too—in squadrons. They were all over the place—in the corridors, along the boards and even up in the stands with the fans! I didn't like the looks of that.

The players came out to warm up, Djurgårdens in their mainly white uniforms, absolutely covered with advertisements, and AIK in mostly black, looking equally like moving billboards.

The crowd went wild. So wild it was freaky. It felt like the whole Globe was rocking, and as the two ends of the rink swayed, covered in enormous team banners that looked like the world's two biggest flags, I started to get scared.

Then it got a lot worse.

Just as the players left the ice, a riot broke out at one end. I'm not sure why; maybe the opposing team's fans had gotten into that area. Soon there was a massive fistfight going on, and then the police waded into it, bearing their riot sticks and whacking people. The whole arena started whooping, and I actually reached out and put my hand on Grandpa's arm. The fight seemed to be spreading, coming our way. It had an end-of-the-world, chaotic feel to it, like something really bad was approaching and we were going to be pulled into it and die in this violent crowd whirlpool.

But when I looked up to see Grandpa's reaction, he was laughing.

"Ah, yes, the unemotional Swedes," he said.

"Shouldn't we leave?" I asked, and I'm guessing my face was *really* white this time. He looked down at me, a little startled. Then he smiled. For a second I thought he was going to tell me that I was too sensitive. "It'll be all right," he said with a warm expression. "Just watch."

Sure enough, within moments the police, who were dressed in blue with a little yellow (of course) and wore what looked like bullet-proof vests across their chests, had everything in order. They'd removed the few bad guys and the arena was calm again—or, at least, back to roaring for the game to start.

It was a fast-paced match, the crowd was really into it, and I found it pretty entertaining. Not nearly as much hitting as in an NHL game and not a single scrap, but different and more wide open.

Partway through the third period I could feel that I was getting close to needing to pee. It wasn't surprising, given that Grandpa had bought me not only all the ice cream and popcorn I could eat but also jumbo drinks.

But the game was close, Djurgårdens leading by a goal and AIK pressing, and I didn't want to leave the rink. I hoped I could time it so the two of us could go to the men's room together after the game ended. But with three minutes left, my bladder felt like a lacrosse ball about to explode.

"I need to go," I told Grandpa.

"Go where?" he asked, looking at me as if there was something wrong with me.

"To the washroom."

"Oh, that, sure." He turned back to watch the game. He's a Canadian, and he didn't want to miss a minute.

"On my own?" I asked.

"Sure," he said and looked back at me and then at the game again. "Why not? Remember what I said about growing up, Adam, getting a little older? Surely you can make your way to the washroom. There's one in the corridor right at the top of the stairs here. They have little signs, you know. They're universal…a man and woman? Don't go to the girls' one." He smirked and smacked me on the shoulder and then put his full attention on the game.

It took me a while to get up. But I had to do this…or pee my pants. As I walked up the aisle, Grandpa called out to me, but as he did, the crowd erupted in a huge roar and I looked down and saw that AIK had scored—a beauty goal, apparently "top shelf," as someone screamed out in English. Half the people went nuts, and it was deafening. I looked at Grandpa, and he shouted something at me. I couldn't hear it. But it could wait. I'd be back in a few minutes.

But I wasn't. Out in the corridor, I couldn't find the washroom right away. It certainly wasn't right at the top of the stairs as Grandpa had said, so I had to walk down the hallway a fair distance. I started getting a little anxious, unsure if I could find my way back, but finally I located a little blue-and-gold man sign. There was a bit of a lineup inside, which surprised me. I imagined the clock ticking down on the game, and before I even got up to the urinal, I heard the arena thunder again and the sounds of Djurgårdens supporters chanting. Their team must have scored in the dying seconds. I rushed over to the sink and washed my hands and then raced out into the corridor.

It was full of people streaming out of the arena. The game was over!

I moved as fast as I could, but there were tons of fans on all sides of me and many had had too much to drink and weren't looking where they were going, so it was hard to get past them. It seemed like it took forever to get to our staircase. In fact, it felt like the kind of dream I often have where I'm trying to do something or get somewhere and I can't because things keep getting in my way, delaying me, and I grow terrified.

I wasn't totally terrified yet, but my heart rate was increasing and I could feel fear invading me like something was being dumped in my stomach, something hot.

Finally, I reached the top of our stairs and hurried down them, past exiting fans, until I came to our row.

Grandpa wasn't there.

EIGHT

I couldn't believe it. I stumbled along our row to our seats, which were right in the middle, and just stood there for a while, my heart really banging. I sat down. Grandpa must have just gone out for a minute, maybe to the washroom (though I hadn't seen him out in the corridor), and he'd likely be back any second. But I waited for a long time, what seemed like ten or fifteen minutes (though maybe it wasn't nearly that long), and he didn't come.

It was the worst feeling in the world, absolutely indescribable, like everything had come crashing down.

I started to panic, and I made a bad decision. When I was little, my parents told me that if I was ever separated from them in a public place, I should stay exactly where I was and they would find me. But at this minute, I was separated from Grandpa in a huge crowd in a foreign country. I had to find him—*now*! I ran up the stairs and out into the corridor.

I couldn't see him anywhere. I raced around the entire area, circling the building and searching all the washrooms. Then I made a really bad decision.

I went outside.

NINE

And that was how I found myself standing in that crowd, not a single face familiar to me for as far as I could see, my lifeline cut, fear making my knees weak, and my heart pounding like a basketball rattling hard inside a hoop. I thought back to those *safe* moments a few days before, when I was on the plane with Grandpa by my side.

I was alone. I had *never* been so alone. And I'd never been so frightened in all my life.

TEN

The square was packed with people flowing in all different directions, heading for the subways, hanging out in groups, chanting, bumping into each other, blocking my view of everything. It was hopeless. I'd never be able to spot Grandpa out here. I had to go back inside.

But when I tried to open one of the doors, a burly security guy said something harsh to me in Swedish.

"I have to get back in," I told him in English, alarmed at how shaky my voice sounded, as if I was about to cry.

"You cannot return into the Globe," he said sternly and stood in front of me with his arms crossed.

"But I have to."

"Ticket?"

Grandpa had both of them.

"I don't have one."

"Go away," he said, and he meant it.

I staggered back out into the square. *What was I going to do?*

My first instinct was to stay there, so I leaned against the wall near the door where I'd come out, which was closest to our seats. I peered into the crowd, examining everyone, looking for Grandpa's distinctive old-but-strong-and-erect frame and his beret and white hair. I recalled what he'd been wearing: runners (believe it or not), black jeans (believe it or not) and a red jacket over a black T-shirt. But I couldn't see him anywhere. I was beyond frightened, and my heart hadn't stopped thudding for a long time. I couldn't just stand there anymore. *But what could I do?*

Perhaps I could just speak to a policeman or a security guard or another arena employee. Or even just to an ordinary citizen. But the guy I'd encountered at the door hadn't been too friendly, and the policemen, all in riot-ready gear and looking a little tense, weren't the sort you just walked up to and had a lovely chat with. Though most Swedes seemed to speak English, who knew if these guys did, and maybe I'd say something wrong and get in trouble, and maybe they'd haul me off to jail or something. That didn't make a lot of sense, but what did in Sweden? I'd seen and read too much not to know that people here were full of surprises. I really didn't want to talk to anyone. It might make things even worse. So I put off all those options. I'd just try my best to find Grandpa first. I'd talk to the cops if things got absolutely desperate.

But things actually *did* feel that way, *right now*.

I staggered out into the thinning crowd and stood right in the middle of everything, pivoting around 360 degrees to see as much as I could possibly see. As I turned, the same person kept coming into view at one end of the square.

Someone was watching me.

But it wasn't Grandpa or a policeman or even a creep. It was that orange-haired girl with the ponytails.

She was standing about a hundred yards away, holding on to the bicycle with the handlebars made up to look like a horse's head. And there was a monkey on her shoulder. I'm not kidding. The girl was wearing very weird clothes—a yellow top, a bright-green dress, pink-and-white-striped leggings and black boots that looked way too big for her. She was about my age.

Then she started walking toward me. I was hoping she was going to pass on by, but she kept coming and then stopped when she was right next to me, and I mean *right* next to me. We were eyeballing each other—I think I'm going to be a pretty good size, since Mom and Dad are, and so is Grandpa, but I hadn't started my growth spurt yet. This girl was about my height but very skinny. Her head was less than two feet from mine. Maybe she was one of those close talkers. She had green eyes, and they were sparkling. The monkey on her shoulder said something. It sounded like "*Yip!*"

"You're lost, aren't you?"

Two things surprised me about what she said: first, that she understood my situation, and second, that she knew I wasn't Swedish and spoke English. Was it my black hair, the confused look in my eyes? But many foreigners could look like that.

"No," I said.

"That's a lie."

"No, it isn't."

"My name is Greta Longrinen. What's yours?"

"Bunny," I said.

"That's a lie too. No one is named Bunny… other than bunnies."

"Adam," I said, and my voice sounded really shaky.

"You're scared."

"No. Go away."

"You're an American. I've met lots of them. I've even met some American boys who were lost, and all of them were just like you, very stubborn and afraid to admit that they were scared. Boys are generally like that. They're idiots."

"And who are you, chief of the find-the-lost-boys police?"

"No," she said. "That would be ridiculous."

That stopped me for a second. "I didn't mean that for real."

"And how was I supposed to know that? You said it, didn't you?"

I'd encountered a fruitcake.

"Who are you attempting to locate; and where are you residing whilst living in the environs of Stockholm, Sweden?"

"That's none of your business." I was not only getting sick of her but also wondering if she was working for some sicko, some guy who sent her off to pick up boys and draw them back to his house. She looked enough like a street person. Maybe she'd been watching me since I

71

came to Stockholm. Maybe she was part of the underbelly of Swedish life, innocent-looking on the outside, full of dark intent inside, a perfect character for a Stockholm crime novel, a kid who picks up other kids for some masterminding weirdo. There was no way I was going anywhere with her or doing anything she said.

"Huh?" she said.

"I'm not lost, and even if I were, I can find my own way back to where I'm staying. Just leave, and if you follow me and try to take me away to someone's place, I'll tell the police."

A smirk came across her face. "I don't talk to the cops—most kids don't. They are a bit scary, and lots of us are afraid of them. With good reason."

"I…I don't believe you. Go away or I'll report you as…as someone who is harassing me."

She scrunched up her nose and looked at me in a funny way. So did her monkey.

"I see it's time for a proper introduction." She stuck out her hand. I hesitated and looked at it to make sure she didn't have a weapon. But when

I took it, it was soft and cool. She smiled at me. "I live alone, but don't tell anyone. My mother died when I was young, and my father disappeared about a year ago, though I'm sure he is coming back. We lived on an island in the Baltic Sea, but he had an apartment in downtown Stockholm, so I went there when he went away. I get all these government checks addressed to him, and I forge his signature on them and use them to survive. I even pay my own rent."

"No you don't. That's all a lie."

"Isn't!" she said and raised her chin and stared at me. "You can ask the admiral here if I'm telling the truth."

"Yip," said the monkey.

"I don't worry about anything, absolutely nothing, unlike you, Mr. Adam. You seem sort of sensitive to me."

I couldn't believe it.

"I'm going now," I said, though I had no idea where and I knew it wasn't a good plan to leave the square.

"Tell me where you're heading and I'll guide you," she said and took me by the hand. "Let's make it an adventure! Let's pretend we're explorers!"

I shook her off. Swedish girls were obviously pretty bold.

"I'll do this on my own, thank you very much."

She smiled. "All right, I'll watch. On your way!"

I hesitated. I wasn't even sure which direction to go. I couldn't get on the subway, because Grandpa had our return tickets and I didn't have a dime in my pocket. And, of course, I didn't have a cell phone. If I left here, which wasn't even a good idea in itself, I was going to have to walk all the way back to the hotel through suburban Stockholm and then the southern part of the downtown area, and it was growing dark. I figured it was at least a three-mile trip...if I went the right direction...and didn't get killed on the way.

We stared at each other for a while, and then I started to move.

"Wrong way."

"How do you know? You have no idea where I—"

"Well, unless you are staying in Denmark, I think you should head north, back into central Stockholm."

Central Stockholm—land of secrets, of assassinated prime ministers, sports thugs, riot police who kids feared and happy people who seemed harmless but committed crimes worthy of dark novels. I was going to go there as the sun set, twelve years old, all alone. But I couldn't let her know that I was afraid. I'd just go a bit north and then double back, wait here in the square, speak to a cop. They couldn't be that bad— they were cops, after all. Grandpa must be here somewhere.

But the girl followed me, riding her horse bike with that monkey on her shoulder. I couldn't shake her, though, to be honest, I didn't think much about her at first because I was so anxious about not getting even more lost. Guys are supposed to have a pretty good sense of direction (which I certainly hadn't shown at first, heading off toward Denmark), so I tried to just feel my way. I wasn't going far anyway. I remembered Grandpa pointing out the direction of the Baltic Sea and Russia when we were on top of the Globe, and that was to the east. I tried to picture where everything was when we were up there. I glanced up at the SkyView on the Globe. The sun had just set in the west, so I turned and headed under the bridge for the six-lane highway that ran beside Globe City on its way in and out of Stockholm, and went east until that road turned north.

There wasn't much to see at first. Though this was a suburb, there weren't really any houses, just businesses and apartment buildings.

The girl kept following. I didn't know whether she thought she was staying out of sight, but it didn't take much to spot her riding that horse-bike, her bright hair and ponytails and loud clothes clear from far away.

So I couldn't turn back. North and farther north I went, farther from Grandpa. I'd gone maybe nearly a mile along this busy road when I came to a bridge. I realized that if I went over it I'd be a really long way from the arena, and it might not make any sense to turn around. By then I hadn't seen Greta for a while. It was completely dark.

I had to decide. Forward or backward? Neither made much sense. But it seemed like it was best to head for home, the hotel, a landmark I knew existed and wasn't moving.

I ran over the bridge and decided to keep running, to just gamble and make for central Stockholm, which I was pretty sure was straight ahead. I figured if I kept on one of the main roads, I would soon get to the Old Town, the Gamla Stan, and from there it would be easy to find the hotel. I hadn't seen any police for a while anyway.

I must have run for ten minutes after I crossed the bridge, moving along a wide busy street that still had lots of people on it, a commercial area with storefronts at street level, set in four- and five-story buildings. I saw McDonald's and Pizza Hut and Starbucks as well as cooler places. I was like a cannonball being fired straight north up this long route toward the area where I thought I'd find our hotel. I tried not to make eye contact with anyone and noticed lots of sketchy people, but I have pretty good wheels and just kept burning forward, not giving anyone a chance to consider that I was a kid all alone.

After a while, though, everything started looking wrong to me. Why wasn't I getting to the next bridge, the one that led off this island and into Gamla Stan? What if I were going the wrong way, moving as fast as I could *away* from safety? Could I somehow have gotten turned around? I kept running, but it seemed to me that I had gone nearly another mile and yet there was *still* no end in sight, no bridge, no Old Town.

It didn't make any sense. Then I saw a subway station tucked into a building at street level, cement steps with silver railings going downward, surrounded by green-tiled walls and huge ads for clothes and electronic devices.

What if I went down there? If I just had a ticket, I could go right into the Metro, find a map on a wall, figure out which direction to take and then do it. Getting around on the Green line had seemed pretty simple when Grandpa and I were on the train. I'd checked it out. If I could simply go the right way on the subway, I'd be back at the hotel in no time. I knew the central station downtown was called T-Centralen, and I knew I could navigate my way back to our hotel from there or from a subway station near it. It would be easy.

But I *didn't* have a ticket.

Then I remembered that it didn't seem like there were always attendants next to the entry areas to the platforms. What if I sneaked in and somehow got past the turnstiles?

What if they caught me?

I stopped for a second and stared at the entrance. A man came to a sudden halt nearby and eyed me.

I descended.

ELEVEN

I went down the steps three at a time, my heart back in pounding mode. It was getting darker as I went, like I was descending into you-know-where. There were lots of people in front of me but no one behind. I got to the bottom quickly and then noticed that someone was following me: the guy who had stopped and looked at me on the street above. It seemed like it was only him behind me, like I'd entered the subway at a moment when there were few people about, like a bubble in the crowds. I hurried toward the row of turnstiles.

The turnstiles were upright silver steel boxes with clear plastic things like the swinging doors in a saloon. You had to insert your ticket (which I did *not* have) into a slot in one of the boxes and that would momentarily open the doors so you could enter. I saw lots of people going through them in front of me.

Then I saw something *really* bad. There was an attendant watching everyone entering!

But I had to do this. I couldn't turn around, not back toward that solitary guy who had looked so closely at me on the street, blond and unshaven, dead blue eyes—a perfect killer in a Swedish crime novel.

The crowd in front had gone through, and I was alone for a moment. I glanced at the attendant. He was looking away, his attention taken by something in the other direction.

I leapt over a turnstile!

Then I kept running. I didn't turn around for a second, and I didn't hear anyone shout. I was in!

This was one of those truly awesome Stockholm stations. I remembered reading on Mom's laptop that this subway line was like the world's longest art gallery, filled with incredible cave-like areas painted in striking colors, all with different themes.

I checked a map on a wall and found which platform to go to—just three stops to my destination—and then went down the long gleaming silver escalator, descending into the most breathtaking cave I'd ever laid eyes on. I doubt I'll ever see anything like it again. It was deep red, and the surface kind of hung from the ceiling like lava from a volcano, as if it could drip on you. There were streaks of black in it, and it all glowed, almost as if you were in… you know where. I had been running down the escalator but I stopped hurrying for a moment and just took it in, which was a mistake. One of those silent trains had pulled up while I stood stock-still on the moving escalator, staring at the ceiling. People had quickly filed onto the train, nice and orderly like good Swedes, and by the time I looked over at it, the doors had all quietly closed.

I stepped off onto the floor in that blood-red cave as the train pulled out, and I was all alone. You could have heard a Swede breathe. I looked up the escalator to see the guy who had been behind me. And he wasn't there.

I stood between the tracks in that dead silence in that bizarre place and started to freak out. I remembered how long it had taken the train to come when Grandpa and I were waiting at the station.

I stood there forever. The silence continued. No train came. Then I started to worry that it was getting late and the trains had stopped running. But it wasn't late, although it was dark outside. Then I became concerned that they'd seen me jumping the turnstile on a subway camera and they'd shut everything down and were coming to get me. But that was ridiculous, and I couldn't hear anyone. Not a single person. Not a single sound.

Wasn't *that* weird? What was going on?

I kept waiting. Nothing happened. Then the ceiling and the red lava walls looked like they were moving! But that was impossible too. I realized that I was *really* freaking out.

And then the guy who had been following me emerged from the shadows in the cave, about thirty feet away, and started walking toward me!

I turned and ran.

TWELVE

The escalator was about half a football field away and I made for it at a speed I'd never traveled before. And when I got there, I didn't wait for it to move me. I raced up four rising steps at a time. On the next floor, I ran for the turnstiles. The attendant was right there, and this time he was looking directly at me!

But I didn't hesitate. I leapt over the turnstile and kept moving! I heard him shout something in Swedish, and then his footsteps were coming rapidly after me. I turned a corner and hit the stairs up to the street, breathing hard, taking as many as I could manage at a time, and in an instant, it seemed, was back out on the street with the smells of the city wafting over me. The sky was pitch black and all the street lights had come on. Back at the same intersection, I turned up the street I'd been on and kept running, in and out of the scattered groups of pedestrians, barely missing people, heading in the direction of Gamla Stan and the hotel.

Or at least I thought I was.

I ran for another five minutes, and no one seemed to follow me. But nothing familiar came into view. So I kept running, at least five minutes more, and it was only then, when I was nearly exhausted, that I saw it, the most welcome sight I'd witnessed since I left America: an old bridge, and across it the ancient buildings of the Gamla Stan! I was getting closer to home, maybe just another ten minutes away! Huffing and puffing, I slowed down.

But it was dark now, and those small streets that wound through the Old Town like little alleys through a maze were still between me and home.

It wasn't so bad at first. There was a wide avenue that turned to my left—northwest, it seemed to me—and went along the water as if it were going to wind around the entire little island that made up the Old Town. The old buildings on the other side of the street formed an outer wall for the island about four- or five-stories high, and most seemed to have either restaurants or little stores at street level. People were walking around, looking much more casual than in the commercial area I'd just come from, more relaxed. That was a good thing, and it helped me calm down a little—I kept telling myself, almost arguing with myself, that I was getting closer and closer to the hotel.

Where was Grandpa?

I kept moving along this curving road, just walking now, though at a brisk pace and not making eye contact with anyone, my chest still heaving. A big cathedral appeared on my left and then the road turned away from it and the water a little, and something came charging toward me from behind, rumbling like some sort of monster. I swung around and saw a subway train coming up from underground and moving through a kind of cement corridor behind a cage, like a big snake emerging out of the underworld. I froze for a second and let it sprint past me.

I'm not sensitive.

I kept moving. But then I started getting worried again. And I made another bad decision.

It seemed to me that the road I was on was moving farther and farther to the left, away from where I needed to go, and there was no guarantee that it was going to turn the right way at any point. Maybe it didn't go around the Gamla Stan island and end up on the north side where I had to be. But I was scared to go into the narrow alleyways of the Old Town.

I hadn't seen any police for a long time, nor had I seen Greta, but ever since I'd left the subway—in fact, since I'd left Globe City—it had seemed to me that I was being followed. It was a creepy feeling. I put it out of my mind—it was just me making things up.

It was getting really dark now, and up ahead it seemed even darker. There was more light, and more people and tourists, in the area closer to the buildings. It seemed safer over there. So I crossed the street and walked along the other side, right beside the narrow streets of the Old Town. At each corner I peered into the cobblestoned alleyways. It seemed to me they went directly across the island as the crow flies, right toward central Stockholm and the Grand Hôtel. The little streets seemed better lit than I'd imagined, and there were crowds of people on them. What if I took a chance and went into the maze and moved straight across the island, a shortcut to the hotel? Surely as long as I kept going in the same direction, I'd come out on the other side near the palace, just minutes from home. It really seemed to me that if I stayed on this bigger street, I'd keep going in the wrong direction, farther away from home as it got later and later. I started panicking and ground to a halt.

I turned down one of those narrow streets.

It was like being in a tunnel, but as I walked along the two-foot-wide cobblestone sidewalk it seemed okay at first. I was passing harmless-looking people, many walking in the middle of the street, who barely even noticed me. There were all kinds of cafés and even little stores that were still open and lots of sounds too—people's voices and music. But one thing was missing: children, kids. I was alone with thousands of adults in the alleyways of the Old Town late at night.

Then the little street I was on came to end—a T. I had to choose which way to turn. Or should I go back? I paused for a while and then went to my left, choosing the alleyway that appeared to have the most people and the most light and went in kind of the right direction. But then it ended too, and I had to make another choice.

It was making me dizzy. The streets seemed to be getting even narrower.

My situation reminded me of video games where you went into tunnels or caves or a jungle or through the streets of some sort of futuristic or apocalyptic city in pursuit of bad guys, or when you were being chased, unarmed, twisting and turning for your very life.

I was beginning to worry about my very life for real. The last street I'd chosen was the narrowest yet and had the fewest people. There weren't many restaurants or stores and there were lots of locked doors, some with big steel padlocks.

"Should I turn around?" I asked myself out loud. "Try to find my way back, start all over?"

I was sweating, and my stomach was burning. Greta had long since vanished. The sense that someone was following me had gone. There were a few people half a block in front of me, but there was no one behind me at all.

I stopped and looked straight up into the night sky. I could barely see it in the tight opening between the roofs of the buildings, so I couldn't locate any stars to guide me, to tell me which direction I might go.

I realized I not only had absolutely no idea which way was north—or south or east or west— but also had no sense of which way I had come from. I was utterly and totally lost.

I lowered my head and looked up and down the alleyway. Now I was completely alone. But only for a moment. Someone was approaching, a dark figure, large and male, wearing a hood.

THIRTEEN

I turned and ran, back the way I'd come and then down another alleyway and then another and another, frantically searching and listening for people, for any other living thing. Soon I encountered a few tourists and then a few more. But it wasn't enough. I wanted the safety of a crowd. Going around another corner I ran into someone carrying a drink, and it spilled all over my *I Love Stockholm* T-shirt. He said something that sounded like a Swedish swearword and then started yelling at me. I apologized without looking him in the eye, keeping enough distance between us so he couldn't grab me, and got away.

But just around the next corner I slipped as I tried to make a quick turn and fell face first onto the cobblestones. There was something gross on the ground. I didn't know what it was, but I figured it was what had made me fall. It smelled awful, so maybe it was dog poop—there were lots of dogs in Stockholm. I picked myself up and noticed that my shirt was torn and so were my pants, the hole that had ripped open exposing my knee and some blood. I wiped myself off, rubbed my hand across my eyes to stop the tears and again raced on, down one alleyway after another, out of my mind with panic.

Finally, I stopped near a group of restaurants and a crowd of people. I leaned against a wall and took in great gulps of air, trying to stop the fear that had been fueling my flight, pressing my head against the cool stone surface, telling myself that I was safe now.

When I had calmed down a little, I lifted myself off the wall and stood up straight. I opened my eyes and looked along the street I was on, way along it, and I thought I saw a girl on a bicycle in the distance. I couldn't tell if it had a horse's head, but it seemed that she was looking back down the street toward me. Then she moved on. And when she did, I saw something heavenly behind her— open space and beyond it the purple-brown walls of the royal palace!

I started running again, this time exhilarated rather than afraid, and before I knew it emerged on the wide street at the south end of the palace and into freedom. There was the harbor to my right! There were lots of lights and scores of people and boats easing along nearby and, across the water, the outline of the one and only Grand Hôtel!

"YES!!" I cried out, not caring who heard me. I started at a quick pace for my destination, turning at the front of the palace and walking along the water, then over the bridge and then right along the north side of the river toward the front doors of the hotel.

By the time I got close, I was much more relaxed, moving slowly and feeling very grown up. It was like Grandpa had said to me: I was getting older, capable of more things, and it wasn't so bad to have your capabilities tested. I'd passed. Man, would I have lots to tell him. I had the feeling that though he'd be freaked-out by all of this, he'd be pretty proud of me too.

But the doorman gave me a funny look as I approached the door, and when I put my hands out for it, he reached for me and said something in Swedish. I didn't think it was a swearword, but it wasn't very pleasant either.

I turned my shoulder like I'd often done in baseball when running down the third base line trying to avoid a catcher's tag while heading for home. I guess this doorman hadn't played much baseball, because he totally missed me. But I wasn't going to wait around for him to catch up. I bolted up the steps and into the lobby and made for the golden elevators across the room. But a bellman, or maybe the concierge, saw me coming and tried to block my way.

What was going on? But I'd forgotten what I looked like. I was filthy, my shirt covered in some alcoholic drink and caked with grime, my pant leg was ripped open at the knee, where I was bleeding, my face was dirty, and of course… I smelled like dog poop.

I turned and made for the reception desk. These guys would recognize me, wouldn't they? They'd surely seen me before.

But the guy on duty didn't look familiar, and as I ran up to him he barked something in Swedish at me. I wasn't sure if it was a swearword too, but it definitely could have been.

"I'm staying here," I stuttered, "with…with my grandfather…David McLean!"

"Take him out of here!" cried the man behind the desk in English, glancing up and down the lobby, looking embarrassed. In an instant, two bellmen had me in a grip and were ushering me toward the main doors.

"You can't do this! I AM STAYING HERE WITH MY GRANDFATHER!" I shouted.

"Not anymore," said one of the big blond bellmen with a grin as they shoved me out onto the street.

Now I was lost *and* homeless.

FOURTEEN

That was when I broke down. I couldn't take it anymore. I staggered across the broad street in front of the hotel and over the wide sidewalk to the steel-tube fence that ran along the edge of the water, where people stood to take in the spectacular view of the palace and the older town. And I started to cry.

I buried my face in my hands and didn't look up for a long time. But after a few minutes I felt my grandfather's hand on my shoulder…not his real hand. I imagined it.

I thought about what he would say if he were here beside me. He'd tell me to get ahold of myself, to get off my butt and find a way to locate him, no matter how impossible the situation might seem. I straightened up. I had passed a number of policemen since I'd crossed the last bridge, and there were several within sight right now. I should go into a restaurant, a fast-food place, there were American ones here, and go to the washroom and clean myself up and then find a cop and speak to him in a clear, mature voice and convince him that I wasn't a street kid and that I needed help. Wouldn't he help someone like that? But the terror I'd been feeling started invading me again. What if he wouldn't listen? I was in deep trouble in this foreign city. I dropped my head again and fought myself, trying not to collapse. This is stupid, I told myself. Just talk to someone, *anyone*—they'll help you. Then I felt a real hand on my shoulder. It was smaller than Grandpa's and gentler.

"Mr. Adam?"

I looked up and saw Greta, the weird girl, peering at me. I pretended to notice something across the water and turned my face toward it, running my hand quickly across my eyes and wiping them as best I could.

"Were you crying?"

"No."

"You're awfully sensitive."

"*Stop* saying that!"

"I only said it twice!"

"I'm not crying. It's windy out here. The wind is in my eyes."

"Sure," she said, popping up the stand on her bike and then leaning against the railing with me, looking out across the water as if we were together or something. The monkey stared out with us, one of the gang. None of us uttered a word for a while. All we could hear were the sounds of Stockholm…and maybe my pounding heart.

"*I'm* not a crier," she said suddenly. "Haven't cried once, ever."

"That's a lie."

"Well, maybe once or twice, but not very often. I bet you don't believe that."

"I don't care."

"I bet you think all girls are criers. If I went around crying all the time, I'd be in deep trouble. In fact, I'd be dead." She smiled. It was a pretty goofy smile, wide and genuine, framed by that red hair and ponytails, and it almost made me smile back. I looked away quickly.

"I really don't care," I said.

"You should never judge a book by its cover or a girl by her appearance." She paused for a few seconds and smiled again. "Hey, that's pretty good."

"Not bad," I said.

"I hope you don't grow up to be one of those guys who judges girls by their looks. A lot of guys turn out that way, and it sucks. It's what's inside that matters, you know. Character...that sort of thing."

"Aren't you the philosopher."

"No, I'm not a philosopher, I'm a kid, and I plan to grow up to be the prime minister of Sweden, or maybe the secretary-general of the United Nations. I don't think being a philosopher would pay well."

"I didn't mean that you actually were."

"Well, you said it."

Wow, what a fruitcake.

"So are you going to spend the rest of the night here, leaning against the fence crying?"

"I wasn't crying!"

"Man, you really are sensitive."

I started walking away, but she kicked up the stand on her bike and followed me, her monkey shrieking and pointing at me as if to say, *He's getting away! Follow him!*

"I've got a dare for you," she said.

"Go away."

"I bet you are going to stay around here somewhere and eyeball the hotel until whomever it was you were with, some adult, comes back and saves you. Failing that, you'll give up and with a trembling heart ask some other adult, some stranger, to solve everything for you. Who are you with? Who is your knight in shining armor?"

"It's my grandfather, David McLean, and what if I am waiting for him?"

"It's boring, and what if he never comes back? What if he has abandoned you?"

A bolt of terror shot through me. I wished she would just shut up.

"He'll be back. He has to come back."

"Why?"

"Because he cares about me and because he came here with me and will, you know, kind of notice that something seems to be missing. I'm sure he's frantic and out there somewhere"—I looked at the city—"desperately searching for me."

"People who are close to you and loving you sometimes just disappear," she said in a lower voice, almost as if she were saying it to herself.

I tried not to look petrified. What if Grandpa had really done that? Why had he brought me to Sweden in the first place? I thought about all the meetings he'd had, visiting mysterious "friends."

"It's absurd to wait around here," said Greta. "You're only doing it because you are afraid. You could never live on your own like I do."

"Yes, I could."

"Then prove it. Here, I'll give you a few kronor," she said, and she reached into her pocket and brought out some colorful Swedish money. "See if you have the courage to go off on your own into Stockholm for a while, just a while, and buy a meal, and survive, like I do... like a girl."

I looked down at the money and then up at her face, which was set in a hard expression, her lips held tightly together, her eyes narrowed.

"You can't do it, can you?"

I paused for a second and then swiped the money out of her hand and walked in the direction of downtown Stockholm, away from the hotel and the Gamla Stan and everything that provided me with even a touch of comfort, including Greta Longrinen.

FIFTEEN

At first I didn't even look behind me. I just kept walking away from the hotel, along the wide street that curved around the water in front of the spectacular old buildings that seemed to be guarding modern downtown Stockholm. But I knew she was following me. I could feel it. And when I got to a square (well, really more of a round) with a statue of some guy, probably a king, on a horse, I glanced back and saw her advancing behind me like she was James Bond or someone, keeping an eye on me. Maybe I should have picked up my pace and lost her at that point, but something inside me didn't want to—*she* was my only lifeline now.

I had some idea where I was going, since Grandpa and I had gone this way in the early afternoon when we were looking for gifts and souvenirs in the trendy shopping area not far from here. So I turned up one of those streets, a kind of walking promenade, though it was wide enough for cars, with gray blocks for the road surface. There were lots of people around, which was a relief to me. Even though it was nearly ten o'clock, quite a few of the little stores were open as well as all of the restaurants and pubs, and there was still lots of noise spilling out onto the street. People went casually past on bicycles. I couldn't believe how many bikes there were in Sweden—they were everywhere. I pulled up against a wall between two cafés and looked back. I couldn't see Greta in the crowd behind me now, though that didn't mean she wasn't there. I walked on, feeling like I was being followed—not necessarily by Greta, just by someone, by something—but every time I turned around, there didn't appear to be anyone in pursuit.

I was getting awfully hungry, but I didn't want to buy anything, didn't want to have to speak to anyone, make myself visible and draw attention to the filthy lost boy whom they might report to the police. I knew that was crazy, but it was what I was thinking. I passed several policemen, several of whom seemed to be eyeing me, but I didn't look at them and kept moving on. Now, I had no idea where I was going. I just knew that I had to be gone for a while—I didn't want to go running like a baby back to the hotel and find Greta there, Muscles herself, laughing at me.

I walked farther north along the promenade than Grandpa and I had and came to a busier street, four lanes wide and lined with big modern buildings, some of which looked like huge department stores, others like banks. There was another square, or round (they seemed to like their squares round in Sweden). This one had a weird fountain in the center with white circles in the water and a statue, or a sort of statue (it was more like a tall jagged piece of skinny rock, like a work of art—Swedes were into art), towering in the middle. I walked past it, noticing the names of the streets nearby, which in Stockholm are on white rectangles fastened to the sides of buildings.

Sveavägen.

This was the street the cab driver had taken us along when Grandpa and I had come through the center of Stockholm on our way from the airport to the hotel. At least it was familiar and I could return on it whenever I wanted and get back to the Grand. I turned up it.

It hadn't seemed this wide and intimidating when we'd been on it just a few days ago. When I stared up from the sidewalk I could see that the buildings here were really tall—fancy, modern apartment buildings and other offices with stores at street level, all of them now closed.

There weren't as many people here. In fact, once I was a fair piece along the street it was almost deserted, just the odd person passing me as I headed away from the safety of the hotel and Greta. But I couldn't turn around, not yet.

The sensation that someone was following me dogged me, but every time I turned around there was no one. In fact, often there was literally no one near me, not a soul on the street nearby.

It didn't seem like a good idea to go farther, so I decided to turn around. But then I realized something. The place where Olof Palme, the Swedish prime minister, had been brutally murdered was just a block away.

I don't know why, but something was drawing me there. I wanted to see it and maybe, if I could summon enough courage, actually stand on the very spot. I was imagining what happened that night—the bad guy approaching with his pistol in the darkness as the prime minister and his wife walked along the safe Stockholm street, history and drama about to unfold. I'm kind of interested in guns, though I know that in some ways I shouldn't be. I don't think I'm intrigued in a bad way. It's mostly because they are like little machines, really dynamic, firing objects at amazing speed through space. (The coolest gun is the one James Bond uses—can't remember the name of it though.) By the time I neared the murder scene, it seemed like I was the only one on the street for miles around.

I knew where the location was from the reading I'd done and the fact that I'd seen what I thought was the exact spot when Grandpa and I drove in from the airport. But it was very different to see it on foot and all alone. I approached from the far side of the street and stood across from a subway entrance that went down into a building and then into the underground. There was a sign on the building, one of those white rectangular ones with black writing: *Olof Palmes gata.*

I decided to cross the road…go right up to the spot.

Even though I couldn't see a single vehicle on the street, I looked both ways before I crossed at the light, moving cautiously over the black-and-white-striped pathway. There was a very narrow street right in front of me: *Tunnelgatan.* That was it—the alleyway down which the murderer had fled! He had escaped along that tiny artery into the bowels of Stockholm and forever away, like an elusive villain in a story! At least, that's what was said. I approached cautiously and stood where I figured it must have happened, where the bullet had shot through the night. There was another subway entrance just to my right, a big blue-and-white letter *T* above me and something on the sidewalk to my left, at my feet: a bronze plaque. I stared down at it.

The words were in Swedish, but I recognized the name, *Olof Palme*, and the date, *February 28, 1986*, and it seemed to me that another word, *mördades*, probably had something to do with murder. My hands grew sweaty, and my heart rate picked up. I raised my head and stared down the narrow street. Its name sounded like a tunnel. *Tunnelgatan.* It looked like one too. It seemed to disappear into utter darkness.

I was really good at imagining things, bad things usually—Mom often said that. And right now I was imagining *really* awful things.

I should go home immediately, down Sveavägen to the Grand Hôtel, force them to let me in, find my grandfather and then go all the way home, back to America, to my mother and father. I didn't care whether I was being sensitive or not. Maybe that's what I was. Who cared? I just wanted to go home!

But then I saw a figure coming toward me out of the darkness. And it was running right at me. From where I stood, it appeared to be a man, quite large and dressed in black with short black hair and a mustache—the very likeness of the assassin who had been accused of murdering Palme but had never been convicted. The prime minister's wife, who had been right beside him on that beautiful night as they walked home from a movie in perfect, nonviolent Stockholm and had seen him murdered in cold blood, had picked this person out of a lineup a few years after it happened!

I turned and fled down Sveavägen. But when I was just a few strides farther, I knew it wasn't a good idea to try to run. This man's legs were way longer than mine, and no one was nearby to help me. He would catch me instantly. I slipped into the doorway of the closest building and flattened myself against the wall, trying to calm my breathing, which seemed as loud as the wind in a storm. As I stood there, I wondered where Grandpa was at that very moment—how could he have lost me? What was he doing? What did he do all day at the meetings that he told me nothing about? I imagined how he would feel when they found my dead body lying on Sveavägen, right near the spot where the prime minister was murdered!

I heard the man emerge from the tunnel-like street. He paused for a second, breathing hard, probably looking both ways, searching for any sign of me. Then he started coming my way.

SIXTEEN

He came my way slowly, as if unsure, as if examining every doorway, every building, as he reached it. Then he came even with me and I glimpsed him—or, at least, the side of his head, hair as black as the night. He was staring down Sveavägen in the direction I had originally come from. His shoulders were broad, and his hands, like the thick ends of two clubs, hung down at his side, twitching. It didn't seem to me that he had a weapon, though he could have been hiding it. Guns didn't seem so cool at that moment. I held my breath.

But he walked right past me. And he didn't turn around—at least, not at first. I watched him from my hiding spot, and when he was a good fifty feet away, I stepped out.

That was a mistake.

Just as I moved, he turned around. I didn't see his face clearly because the instant he began to pivot, I was off and running the other way, up Sveavägen. I could hear him starting to accelerate after me.

Where could I go? I was far from the hotel and any sort of safety, and I couldn't see anyone for miles. It didn't make sense to keep fleeing up this big street where he had a clear view of me and could track me. I turned in to the Tunnelgatan. I had no idea where it went, where the assassin had vanished after he slipped into it that horrible night, but that was where I was going. Maybe I could vanish too!

I'd never run so hard in all my life, and once I was ten or so strides in, the tunnel got dark. All the doors in the buildings were slammed shut and likely locked, and up ahead it looked totally black. It felt like I was going back in time too, along a narrow cobblestoned medieval street where Vikings lurked. I came to a cross street and considered taking it, but it was nearly as narrow and almost as dark, so I kept moving forward. I could hear the man behind me, thundering along, breathing heavily and gaining on me!

And maybe he wasn't the worst of my enemies. Maybe he was just driving me in here—a lost boy all alone herded into a dead-end street where a whole gang of thieves and murderers could fall upon me. It struck me as a perfect opening scene in a Swedish crime novel—you see the kid pursued and then gruesomely terminated and then it fades to black and a grim, depressed Swedish detective with all sorts of issues figures out the motivations and the identities of these faceless murderers, these sickos.

Then I spotted a steel gate stretched across the end of the tunnel—no doubt locked, shut down at this time of night because it was too dangerous to go any farther. That was it then. This was the end. My assassin had indeed driven me in here on purpose. But I didn't see any accomplices, and then I spotted something that surprised me even more. Stairs! There were stairs in the middle of the street, running steeply upward on each side of the gate. And beyond them, I could see light! Or at least I thought I could: dim and distant. I raced up the hard stone stairs as if pounding up the steps in a dungeon. It wasn't clear where they were going, but I had no choice. Then there was another staircase, and then another, narrowing toward the center, leading up to who-knows-what!

As I went higher, my legs started to feel like lead and I began to stagger. I was slowing down, *really* slowing down, and I could hear the beast behind me gaining ground. But up ahead, way up another two flights, I still thought I could see that light.

I ascended the next flight and then began to climb the last. I could barely move! I'd started out taking three steps at a time, then two, and now I could barely do one! Finally, I was halfway up the last flight, still ten or more steps to go, looking down at my feet, unable to raise my head to see what was in front of me, grabbing my legs to pull them forward to make each step.

Five steps left! It seemed like the man was just a few strides behind and not slowing. Was he superhuman?

Three steps, then two…then one!

But I stumbled on that last one…and felt a hand reach out and grab me from behind!

I somehow lurched up onto level ground with the hand still on me, trying to push him off, raising my head and seeing that I was on a street, a brighter one.

"Mr. Adam?"

Greta Longrinen was standing there, holding the handlebars of her horse-bike, the monkey on her shoulder.

"Yip," said the admiral.

SEVENTEEN

"You look really scared," she said. "Man, you're white."

"Greta! Run! There's a—" I whipped around and looked down the staircase toward my assassin. There was no one there. It was absolutely empty and silent both on the steps and down in the Tunnelgatan. On the street where we stood, people were passing, talking, laughing, some arm in arm, happy Swedes out on the town, their secrets well hidden.

"A what?" she asked.

Though there wasn't anyone down there now, I was certain someone had been chasing me or at least following me.

"Nothing," I said to her. "I'm fine. I didn't need your money." I reached into a pocket and handed it back to her, even though I was feeling pretty weak and horribly hungry. Maybe my condition had made me hallucinate?

"You didn't eat? What are you, nuts?"

I hadn't wanted to interact with anyone, especially anyone Swedish, which had eliminated a rather large number of options.

"What are you doing here?" I asked her.

"I live nearby."

"Near *here*? Really?"

"Of course. Do you have a problem with that?"

"No, I just thought that maybe—"

"You should go back to the hotel. It isn't entirely safe downtown late at night. Although you know that thing I said about Swedish cops being scary and kids should fear them? Not true. They're great—really kind and nice. I can't believe you fell for that."

"Didn't."

"Yes, you did. Boys are so funny. I knew you'd fall for the challenge to head out into Stockholm alone at night too. Only an idiot would do that."

I didn't know how to respond, but if I was such an idiot, then why was she talking to me, and why had she followed me, and why was she just standing there now, not moving, not going away?

"Well," she said, "I must be leaving. Tallyho!"

"You're lonely."

"No I'm not."

"That's a lie."

"Is it really? Well, just watch me walk away, right now." She didn't move an inch. She was looking at me like she wanted me to say something, tell her she could hang out with me, come back to the hotel and meet Grandpa. As I've said, I'm not really into girls, not yet anyway, though I must admit that lately I've been noticing them a bit. They're kind of neat, in a way, sort of. I was finding myself kind of, almost, checking them out these days. It was weird. But this one was awfully strange-looking. It wasn't her looks that interested me. It was something about her as a person, something behind her eyes. She was, I hate to say it, very interesting.

"Look at this," she said suddenly and grabbed her bike with one hand and lifted it high into the air. Man, she was really strong.

"Yip!!" cried her monkey and raised his hands above his head as if in a cheer.

"That's, uh, that's impressive."

"Think you can do it?"

I didn't want to. Not that I was worried I'd fail—I just didn't want to. I'm not sensitive. I waved her off.

"You know, sensitive isn't such a bad thing," she said, looking at me like she liked me or something, reading my mind. We were making eye contact. I looked away.

"I'm not that."

"Well, I am sometimes. Strong and sensitive, that's me!"

"And modest."

"Nothing wrong with believing in yourself!"

"I've got to get going."

"Sure, go straight down this street in the direction you came from. It's, uh, actually pretty safe. Stockholm is really tame. You should be just fine."

"Thanks…see you later."

"Yeah, later. Sure."

"Bye."

"Bye."

She wasn't moving, so I did. I turned my back on her and started walking away, but then I heard her calling out to me. I turned around.

"Remember me!" she shouted. She was holding her bike high in the air.

Not long after, probably less than a minute, I turned around to see where she was going. But she'd vanished. I stood there and looked in the direction she must have walked or ridden, and for a few seconds I had the silly idea that she had never been there, that Greta Longrinen *truly* didn't exist, never had. I wondered if she was someone I'd invented to give me courage, to push me to be stronger, to deal with my troubles. If so, it was pretty strange that I'd come up with a girl.

There I was, silently talking to myself again. There's definitely a good me and a bad me inside my head, fighting each other to make the right decisions.

But I shook all that off. Greta had to be real. I had been talking to her, hadn't I, a whole bunch of times? And the guy chasing me in the tunnel… he was real too, wasn't he? It was strange though: he hadn't said a word, and I'd never really seen him, not clearly. But man, it had been awfully frightening, as real as the light wind I could feel now on my face as I walked down this busy street toward the hotel.

I'm *not* sensitive.

Soon I was thinking about the hotel and Grandpa. Where the heck was he? Wasn't he searching for me? Were the Grand's employees going to throw me out into the street again? I'd escaped death and now I was heading back to the only place that offered any kind of comfort. But would it?

I'm not...sensitive.

EIGHTEEN

I decided I had to man up and stride into the hotel lobby like I meant business—not take no for an answer, demand my rights, demand to see my grandfather. In order to do that, to pump myself up, I started to think of the way the guys and I got just before we went out onto the ice at the beginning of a game. I imagined a really intense encounter ahead of me, like we were playing Canada, which, unfortunately, was pretty good in hockey. Well, not pretty good—awesome, to be honest, though I would never, *never* tell my cousins that.

Then I imagined that *they* were all on the Canadian side, and my team was heading out to play *them*, and to get myself ready even more I imagined going one-on-one with each and every one of them right at that very minute. Me against the rest of the McLean family, proving my worth! I figured I could take Bunny, though he isn't exactly small and sometimes surprises you. DJ would be a problem and Steve too, since he's got a bit of an attitude. Webb's got a dark side and might be unpredictable, so I'd have to be ready for him. Spencer? No problem—he'd likely be skating around with a camera in his hand!

I decided to focus on DJ. He'd be the toughest, almost perfect at everything and a pretty big lad to boot. All I had to do was imagine I was going into a corner against him and had to come out with the puck! With that attitude, I couldn't fail.

I moved quickly down the street and got out of the commercial area in no time and then onto the waterfront street to the hotel. It couldn't have taken me more than ten or fifteen minutes.

I was surprised at the short distance I'd walked. Earlier, it had seemed like I'd been going forever, deep into the city's center.

The hotel appeared even more imposing than it had before, big and sophisticated and kind of glowering, very…Swedish. But I imagined the whole building was DJ and walked right through the front doors, moving so fast and intently that the doorman didn't even have time to turn to grab me.

Then DJ was at the front desk. I made for it. The same guy was standing there, blond and large and beginning to frown as he caught sight of me. I didn't care. I needed the puck. I was going to smack him and take it from him!

"Look," I said and was a little shocked to hear that my voice was shaky, "I'm staying here, okay? And you can't send me away. I'M STAYING WITH MY GRANDFATHER, DAVID McLEAN!"

The guy started to open his mouth but no sound came out—at least, not from him. It came from across the lobby.

"Adam?"

I turned around, and the guy behind the desk and I looked in the same direction, out toward an armchair. Someone was sitting in it, a newspaper in hand, assuming the color of the wall, watching what was going on around him, calm like James Bond. He got up and turned to us.

It was Grandpa.

"Adam! Where the heck have you been? I've been searching all over for you." He started walking toward me, arms outstretched. "When I came back to our seats at the rink, you'd gone, my boy!" He clasped me in a warm hug. Man, did it feel good. I just snuggled into him...and tried not to cry.

"Why," I stammered, "why aren't you out in the streets looking for me?"

"I figured you'd gotten someone, maybe a policeman, to take you back here, so I came back as fast as I could. It's only been about an hour or so. I was getting a little worried though."

"An hour or so?" It hadn't seemed like that, and when I looked up at the big clock behind the desk, I could see that it had been a bit longer than that, closer to two hours. Man, he seemed relaxed about it all.

"I knew you could handle yourself. And Stockholm's a pretty safe place."

"No, it isn't," I said quickly. "It's full of crime and shady people and trouble."

He laughed. "Adam, have you been reading my crime novels?"

"No," I said.

"I didn't mean you actually had, my boy, but you've got your imagination going overtime. I guess that's just your way. Sweden is a lovely place, and Stockholm is as safe as any city in the world—much, much safer than Buffalo. The police are very helpful. Any citizen too. I'm sure you asked for help...didn't you?"

"Sure."

"What's with the torn pants and the dirty shirt?"

I was glad his sense of smell was almost gone. War wound, probably.

"Uh, I just slipped. Can we go to our room?"

"Sure. I'll order up some food, some hot chocolate and maybe some popcorn and drinks for later. How about a movie? James Bond?"

NINETEEN

The flight home was horrible. Oh, it was as smooth as sitting on a pillow, no turbulence. That wasn't the problem. It was me. I kept thinking about us plummeting to the ocean far below, our faces distorted as we dropped at gut-wrenching speed, our tragedy a huge story on the news. When was I going to get over this sensitivity thing? It really ticked me off.

The mighty David McLean noticed my unease. I know he did. But he didn't say anything. He just sat there as calm as a monk, reading crime novels and news stories in a series of papers.

"Grandpa, what do you really do on these trips?"

He raised an eye. "*Really do*? What do you mean by that?"

"All that time you spent away from me in the morning, what were you doing? You never once told me anything about it, no details."

He laughed. "Adam, you are twelve years old. What do you think I should do, give you my business itinerary? You know I love to travel, always have, and luckily, I have friends everywhere. I'm blessed. I still like to fly, I like to see old acquaintances, and I still do a few deals." He gave me a wry smile.

"Deals?"

"Business deals. There's still some fight in the old fart, you know." Grandpa was like that, a little salty-mouthed sometimes. Mom had had to rein him in around the cousins more than once, but we all loved it. He was pretty cool.

"You, uh, you seemed awfully calm about me getting lost." That had actually bothered me, even though I hadn't said anything. I wished he'd run up to me and slapped me or something when I turned up at the hotel. Instead, he was just calm and together David McLean, as usual. As I thought more about it, I kind of wanted to scream at him.

"Lean forward," he said to me in a quiet voice. He looked awfully serious. I moved my ear right up to his mouth. "I had my people following you," he whispered. "They were right on your trail the whole time, and there was nothing to be worried about."

I knew it! I hadn't imagined that I was being followed! I pulled back and stared at him. He motioned for me to lean in again.

"And if you believe that, I've got an elephant in my luggage, a real live one, which I caught on Sveavägen when he escaped from a circus, and I'm bringing him home for you to ride up and down the streets of Buffalo and then bring

139

into school for show-and-tell." He turned back and started reading his novel again

I felt like an idiot. Well, not a total idiot, because it was my grandpa who'd just put me on and he never made me feel like I was anything but wonderful. All my cousins felt that way around him too. Who else would take us on a trip like he'd just treated me to? But I did feel a bit silly. And I still wasn't happy about him being so calm about losing me. It was still ticking me off.

"But you were awfully calm, Grandpa... it kind of...kind of upset me."

He stopped reading and looked at me, a big grin on his face. "Good for you," he said. "Give me a shot."

"What?"

"Give me a shot right on the shoulder, your best shot. I deserve it."

My grandfather was asking me to punch him.

"Go ahead."

I let him have one, though I held back a little. After all, he's really old. He took it well, didn't utter a sound, though I think he felt it a bit. He grinned again.

"I was actually pretty upset, Adam—*very* upset. I looked all over for you in the arena and had the police searching for you and let everyone at the Globe know where we were staying and came rushing back to the hotel and gave them a description of you and started searching around the Grand and out into Stockholm. I was so—what's the word you use?— freaked-out that I thought I was going to have a heart attack."

"The guy at the desk didn't seem to get the message."

"Well, I don't think he was looking for a kid with grime on his face and a bloody knee and smelling of alcohol and, uh, poop. That wasn't exactly the description I gave them."

"But you were calm when you finally saw me!"

"I had just been outside, coming back from searching, and was thinking about putting out an alert for you in the city...when I saw you walking back into the hotel, looking kind of dazed, talking to yourself, actually. I sneaked into the lobby behind you and pretended to be reading the newspaper."

"You did? How come you didn't tell me that until now?"

"Tell you all this before? Where is the fun in that?"

I stared at him for a second and then we both broke into a laugh.

"All's well that ends well," he said, quoting somebody, and he gave me a big hug.

We crossed the Atlantic and landed in Buffalo. Mom and Dad were there to meet me, and neither Grandpa nor I said a word about what had happened. It was our secret.

But I had an even bigger secret, one that even David McLean didn't know about—a girl named Greta, real or not.

* * *

Before we parted the next day at our house, Grandpa and I had a farewell hug.

"You really had me going back there in Sweden," I said. "I really thought you hadn't cared that much about me getting lost."

"Well, I did. But in the end, it was good for you. Remember what I told you about growing up. It's time for you to do that. Some troubles aren't a bad thing, even some big troubles, even being in danger and being really afraid. You'll experience it all in life, and how you react to it will determine the kind of man you will become." Then he paused for a second, just before he walked away. "In fact," he said, "it wouldn't have been such a bad thing if I'd abandoned you on purpose for a while. Someday, you know, Adam, I'll be gone."

He gave me a very strange grin, clapped me on the back and walked away.

ACKNOWLEDGMENTS

Thanks go to all the good folks at Orca Book Publishers, who enthusiastically supported the idea, development and creation of Seven (the series) and the Seven Sequels and now our Seven Prequels. It has been quite a ride. First among those at Orca to thank is the boss himself, Andrew Wooldridge, whose dedication this time extends to the brave task of editing all seven novels. Dayle Sutherland and Jen Cameron have also been great allies, instrumental in spreading the word about our wonderful projects. Working with the extraordinarily talented

Gang of Seven—Norah McClintock, Sigmund Brouwer, Richard Scrimger, Ted Staunton, Eric Walters and John Wilson—has been not only an adventure but also educational, both onstage and at the computer! It is great when respected colleagues are also good friends. And final thanks to Sweden, a land much like our own and metaphorically like David McLean—full of secrets.

SHANE PEACOCK is a biographer, journalist, screenwriter and the author of more than a dozen books for young readers, including The Boy Sherlock Holmes series, *The Dark Missions of Edgar Brim* and *The Artist and Me*. His work has won many honors, including the Geoffrey Bilson Award, the Libris Award and two Arthur Ellis Awards for Crime Fiction. His novel *Becoming Holmes* was a finalist for the Governor General's Award. Shane and his wife live with their three children on a small farm near Cobourg, Ontario, where he continues to search for and imagine larger-than-life characters. *Separated* is the prequel to *Last Message*, Shane's novel in Seven (the series).

SEE WHERE ADAM GOES NEXT IN
AN EXCERPT FROM **LAST MESSAGE**
FROM SEVEN (THE SERIES).

MATTERS OF CONSEQUENCE

"He'll never amount to much."

That's what he said. In fact, it was the *last* thing he said about me.

I tried not to resent him as I sat with my mother and father in the gloomy, wood-paneled room in his lawyer's office in Toronto, Canada, fifty floors up in the clouds. It wasn't the appropriate time to resent him, not at all. I very much doubted that anyone else in the room had even remotely similar feelings. He was dead, after all, freshly flown off on his final adventure into the skies, so fit and "with it" that we were all shocked to hear of his death…at age ninety-two.

My aunts, one uncle and five cousins—most of the McLean family, in fact—were gathered around too, restless in big leather chairs. I assumed they were thinking about how great he had been. They were right. I held my bottom lip tightly, though I think it was quivering a little. All three of my aunts had Kleenex in hand, and their faces were pretty red. My Uncle Jerry sat stoically, his mouth in a straight line, and my cousins, all boys, were looking down at the floor or up at the ceiling, not making eye contact with anyone, likely deathly afraid they might start to cry. Even DJ, the oldest grandson (actually only a few minutes older than his twin Steve, but much more mature) who liked to think of himself as kind of the leader of our generation, seemed a little shaky. I think Canadians are a bit wimpy anyway, despite what they can do on the ice.

Mom and Dad looked different. They're really strong people, just like Grandpa, and it showed in their faces. We were the American branch of the family, maybe that was why. We had converted Mom, who was born up here. She was her father's favorite;

everyone knew that, so you'd think she'd be the most upset. But you wouldn't know it if you saw her today. She was holding herself together, looking as calm as I'm sure Grandpa was (Canadian, but no wimp) when he flew one of his missions over France, or as Dad looked the day he landed his American Airlines Airbus at Kennedy Airport on *one* engine, with three hundred passengers on board.

The blinds were drawn in the room, keeping the bright Canadian morning out. Other than the odd sniffle, no one was saying anything. An old, upright clock ticked loudly in a corner.

It wasn't that I wasn't sad. I was. And it wasn't that I didn't love my grandfather. I definitely did. I knew I would miss him hugely, we all would. You'd have to be a robot not to. But I just wished he hadn't said that about me. And I wished it wasn't the last thing I heard out of his mouth. I had enough issues without that…though I think I've hidden them pretty well.

The McLean family was used to getting together for much happier occasions. Grandpa was always the center of things, even when he was really old…

just like today, when you think of it. He never shut up and he never stopped moving. He had a story for and about everything and anything, and they were always well told. But then again, he had a lot to work with—if you wanted to know about being shot at over Nazi-occupied France, sky-high adventures in Iceland, or flying dangerous sorties in Eastern Africa, he was your guy.

I remember the last time we were all in one place, just last summer up near his cottage in the Muskoka Lakes district in the province of Ontario, where lots of movie stars had huge holiday homes. I heard Tom Cruise had property up that way, and (of course) loads of hockey stars summered in those parts too. The cottage was a special McLean place, and we'd had all kinds of fun there over the years. But the high-light for just about everyone but me was the day a few years back when we met in a field near the lake so Grandpa could fly his airplane in and take his grandsons up for a ride. It was one of the last times he flew—one of the final missions in his incredible career. I, uh, remember it all too well.